12-8-08

J
BAY   Baynton, Martin
        Three's a Crowd

DATE DUE

Three's a Crowd

First U.S. edition 2008

Library of Congress Cataloging-in-Publication Data is available.
Library of Congress Catalog Card Number 2007938350

ISBN 978-0-7636-3929-7

10 9 8 7 6 5 4 3 2

Printed in the United States of America

This book was typeset in A Caslon Regular.
The illustrations were created digitally.

Candlewick Press
2067 Massachusetts Avenue
Cambridge, Massachusetts 02140

visit us at www.candlewick.com

Jane and the DRAGON

Three's a Crowd

Martin Baynton

CANDLEWICK PRESS
CAMBRIDGE, MASSACHUSETTS

Cast of Characters

Jane

Brave and headstrong, Jane
is determined to be the first
female knight in the kingdom.

Gunther

A fellow knight-in-
training who often
disagrees with Jane

Rake

The Royal Gardener

Smithy

The Castle Blacksmith

Dragon
Jane's best friend

Pepper
The Royal Cook

Jester
The Royal Court Jester

The King
Cheerful and fun-loving

The Queen
Gentle, kind, and very beautiful

Princess Lavinia
Enjoys being a princess

The Prince
The Royal Brat!

Jane's Mother
Lady-in-Waiting to the Queen

Jane's Father
The King's Chancellor

Sir Theodore
Captain of the Guard

Ivon
A loyal knight

The Merchant
Rich and powerful;
Gunther's father

Chapter One

"Boring!" growled a large green dragon. "Chasing maggots would be more fun than this!" He lay sprawled like a stuffed toy across the castle walls, watching his small friend in the yard below. And he was bored out of his big dragon brain. "Come on, Jane. Stop playing with the clippy-cloppy thing! Time for patrol."

Jane ignored him. She was tired of his complaining. Anyway, it was NOT time for patrol. It was time for jousting practice, and she was trying her best to concentrate. Her young horse, Cleaver, was skittish enough without Dragon spooking him.

Smithy, the stable boy, stood holding Cleaver's lead rein while Jane checked the girth. It was good and tight. The last thing she needed was a loose saddle, not with Squire Gunther watching her every move. He would love the chance to crow at her for some little mistake.

"Jane! Are you planning to ride that horse or buy it?" said Gunther.

"You know the rule, Gunther. 'Check your saddle before the battle.'"

"But there is no battle, Jane. This is a jousting practice. The only danger here is death by boredom."

Jane tried her best not to snipe back at him. Gunther was a complete beef-brain, and it was best to ignore him.

Or beat him. Jane would love nothing

more than to outperform him and wipe
that smug grin from his face. At last
she was ready. She put the toe of her
left boot in the stirrup and swung
herself into the saddle.

A loud and very long fart ripped
through the air. Cleaver shied, threw
back his head, and reared. Jane pushed

her weight into the saddle and kept her seat as Smithy helped calm the horse. Gunther doubled over with laughter.

"Oh, yes. Oh, Jane, your face! Next time you check your saddle, you should check under it!"

Jane dismounted, reached under the saddle and pulled out a deflated pig's bladder.

"Not funny, Gunther."

But Dragon disagreed. Up on the wall, he was laughing so hard, he lost his balance and fell off. The impact shook the flagstones and spooked Cleaver for a second time. The horse pulled free of Smithy and fled back to the stables.

Jane glared at her big green friend. "Dragon, that is not helping."

"Come on," said Dragon with a laugh. "It was funny!"

"It was not. It was childish."

"And funny." Dragon got to his feet

and dusted himself off. "Jane, all you do is practice, practice, practice."

He paused and put one hand under his armpit. "I know! You should practice this." He pumped his arm like a chicken wing.

FAAAAARRRTTTT.

A loud armpit fart sent Gunther and Dragon into a new fit of the giggles.

Jane stared at them for a moment, then headed for the stables. There was no point in talking to Dragon when he was in one of his silly moods. If he wanted to play stupid boy-jokes with Gunther, then he could go ahead. She had better things to do with her time, like brushing poor Cleaver to calm him down.

Chapter Two

*B*rushing Cleaver calmed Jane down too. It was no good being angry when brushing a horse; it just made it more upset. Sir Theodore had taught her that. He had taught her so many skills in the year since she had become his apprentice knight.

Had it been only a year? Jane could hardly believe it. One short year since she had rescued the Prince from dear, silly, annoying Dragon. One year since she had promised Dragon they would be friends for life if he would PLEASE stop stealing little friends to play with.

Jane packed away the grooming brush

and headed to the kitchen for something to eat. She was halfway across Rake's garden when a voice yelled out to her.

"Duck, Jane! DUCK!"

Jane's battlefield training took charge. She dropped to the ground as something whistled over her head and struck the far wall with a wet smack. The gentle face of Rake, the castle's young gardener, emerged from behind a row of cabbages.

"Phew, close one," he said. And he gestured back across the garden.

Dragon stood there, tossing a brown lump from hand to hand as he readied for another throw. At the other end of the pathway, Gunther crouched behind the steps that led to the Royal Gardens.

"Missed me!" yelled Gunther.

"That was only a test shot," Dragon yelled back. "You are going down, short-life! Down, dungy, and dusted."

Gunther emerged from his cover and raced for the protection of a stone archway. Dragon took aim, threw, and hit the wall of the arch.

"Ha! Rubbish!" called Gunther, laughing and ducking through.

"Rake, what are they throwing?" asked Jane.

"Dragon business," said Rake.

"Dragon business? You mean dung? Those two bog-brains are throwing dragon dung?" Jane could hardly believe it. But Rake seemed impressed.

"Yes. Dung bombs. Good for the

garden. DUCK!" They both ducked as another bomb whistled past.

"Dung wars! Are you out of your minds?"

"Jane, there you are." Dragon had

spotted Jane and began patting another bomb into shape. "Yes, dung wars, Jane. And guess who is winning? Big clue: green and impossibly handsome. Come on. Join in. Grab a handful."

Jane stared at him in disbelief. "Dragon, let me think. Erm . . . NO!"

Gunther came running up, his hands loaded with fresh missiles.

"Hold it!" said Dragon. "I have something to tell Jane."

"Does it involve dung?" asked Jane.

"No. Gunther just told me a brilliant joke. Well, not brilliant. Not as completely funny as my own jokes. Do you want to hear it?"

"No."

"So, anyway, there is this knight

fighting a huge army to rescue a damsel in distress. He battles all the way through it to reach her, and he says, 'Eureka!' And then the damsel says, 'Well, you smell pretty bad yourself!'"

Dragon and Gunther fell to the ground in a fit of hysterics. Even Rake started to laugh. But he stopped when he saw Jane's expression, the one she reserved for naughty children and animals.

"Very funny," said Jane. "Now can we go on patrol? Stopping perhaps at the moat to wash your hands?"

"Yes, Dragon," said Gunther, "wash your hands, because you reeka!" And the boys fell down laughing again.

Gunther waved them to silence, lifted his hands to his face, and smelled them. "Wait. Oh, no! I think I reeka too. We both reeka." And again they dissolved with laughter.

"No," said Rake. "I, Raker. You, Gunther."

There was a pause, then the boys all roared again.

Jane stared at them. It felt odd seeing Dragon and Gunther laughing together like this. And she didn't like it. Not one little bit. Dragon was *her* friend, after all. Perhaps Dragon was right. Perhaps she had been too serious lately.

Chapter Three

"Boys can be disgusting pigs!" huffed Jane, pushing a whole muffin into her mouth. She had already finished off three muffins and two glasses of milk since patrol duty.

She was sitting in the Royal Kitchens with Pepper, Kipper Castle's young cook. In fact, Pepper was the only cook, now that the castle had fallen on hard times. At the tender age of twelve, Pepper ran the great kitchen all by herself.

"Pepper?"

"Yes, Jane?"

"Dragon and Gunther seem to be

getting along very well all of a sudden."

"Good," said Pepper. "Everyone should get along."

"I know, Pepper, but those two . . ."

"Those two should be friends, Jane. There are far too many battles and angry words these days. Like they say— there is no coin like a kind word."

Jane sighed. She loved Pepper dearly, but sometimes she was just so . . . so . . . positive!

"Gunther needs good friends, Jane. He has a rough time with that father of his."

"Yes, I know. But why Dragon? And what is so funny about dung and . . . and more dung? I really don't understand."

Pepper laughed and wiped her hands on her apron. "Rake told me a joke the other day. How did it go?

Oh, yes. Who sits on the throne of Gaul?"

Jane shrugged.

"King Louis the Turd!" said Pepper, and she laughed so hard, she had to grab on to the table for support.

"Pepper! Why is that so funny?"

"I have no idea," cried Pepper, and she collapsed into another heap of hysterics.

"I need help," muttered Jane. "I need to try to be more amusing."

After all, she thought, how hard could it be?

Chapter Four

"*P*ut your back into it, you lazy lump!" Gunther's father slammed the side of his wagon with a thick fist. "I want these barrels down at the wharf by noon. Is that clear?"

"Yes, Father."

Besides being an apprentice knight, Squire Gunther was a laborer. He worked for his father, one of the most successful merchants in the village. The man was so successful, the townsfolk called him "the Merchant."

Gunther hauled another barrel of dried herring onto the wagon. The day had turned hot, and he was tired and irritable. "Father, must all these barrels go today? I have duties at the castle."

The Merchant scowled at him. "Your first duty is to me. Now get on with it!"

"But Father, my training is—"

"Training!" The Merchant thumped a barrel. "What do you think pays for your knight's training? This does!" And he thumped the barrel again. "Now, put some effort into it!"

With a groan, Gunther got back to work. A large shadow passed over the street. Gunther looked up. Dragon hovered above him, juggling two large dung balls.

"Hey, Gunther, what's brown and dusty and sounds like a bell?"

Gunther dived for cover as the two missiles hit the wagon, sending dung splattering everywhere.

Dragon flew off, laughing so hard he could hardly keep aloft.

The Merchant stared openmouthed at the filthy mess. "That disgusting reptile!" he roared. "Clean this mess up, boy! Every last bit of it!"

"Yes, Father. But he was only playing."

"Playing! You will not associate with that vile creature! Do you understand me?"

"Yes, Father, but—"

"No buts! I want this lot delivered to the wharf. Every last barrel!" The Merchant turned away and marched into his house. He slammed the door behind him.

Gunther watched Dragon drop out of sight over the castle walls. *If only I could fly off like that,* he thought. With a long sigh, he set to work with a broom to clean up the mess.

Chapter Five

"*You* want to be funny?" said Jester.

"No, Jester. I want to be *hilariously* funny. I want to have Dragon rolling in the dirt. I want to make Gunther laugh so hard, he might bring up his dinner."

"Nice."

Jane grinned. Jester was always the first person she turned to for help. And he was always there for her, with his words of gentle wisdom. It had been Jester who first encouraged her when she told the court of her dream to be a knight.

"But why, Jane? You can handle a sword better than most men. You can ride through the clouds on the back of a dragon. You can even beat the Queen at cards. Why do you want to tell silly jokes? Leave that to those who are a total loss at everything else. Like me."

"Please, Jester. Dragon likes stupid jokes."

"And you worry that he might find you boring?"

"Exactly," said Jane. "I need to be hilariously funny by sundown tonight."

Jester started to laugh. Then he realized that Jane was perfectly serious. "Tonight?"

"Yes, please, Jester. No one makes me laugh like you do. And no one else can walk about in that floppy hat and make it seem dignified."

"Very well. In the face of such shameless flattery, how can I refuse? We shall start at the top with—"

"No. I want to start at the bottom. I want to learn dung jokes. The sort of wet and sticky jokes that make Dragon laugh."

Jester sighed. "I can do dung."

Jane threw her arms around him. "Thank you, Jester!"

"And dung is just the beginning, Jane. Sneezing and vomiting are all good for a laugh. And, of course, farting. Farting is crown king of the low arts!"

"Farting it is!" said Jane. And she tried her hand at an armpit fart. Only a small squeak escaped, but it was a start.

Chapter Six

"Gunther," yelled Dragon. "Do you want to come and chase some cows?"

Gunther looked up to see Dragon coming down for a heavy landing in the village square.

"Go away," he whispered. "I'm busy. I still have to park the wagon around back and . . . and . . . Father will punish me if he finds you here."

But it was too late. The door of Gunther's house opened, and there stood the Merchant. "You again," he growled. "I told you to clear off. Go on; go away."

Dragon glared at the Merchant.

Then he grabbed hold of the empty
wagon and flew off with it.

The Merchant stared in disbelief,
his neck turning an angry red. "Bring
that back!" he roared.

But Dragon ignored him. He flew over the house and disappeared.

Gunther shrank back as his father turned and fixed his anger on him. "What did I tell you? That overgrown worm is nothing but a thief!"

Gunther began to apologize. But he stopped when a heavy thump shook the ground behind him. Dragon had returned.

"Kindly tell your father that his wagon is parked safely in his yard."

"Oh, right. Good," said Gunther, looking from one very red face to one very green one. "Thank you, Dragon."

But the Merchant was in no mood to thank anyone. He turned on his heels and stormed off across the square.

Dragon watched him go and
nudged Gunther. "So, what's big and
sulky and walks like a frog?"

"Shhh, he can hear you," whispered

Gunther. "Come on, I should go before he finds more jobs for me."

And Dragon and Gunther headed back up the cobbled street toward the castle.

Chapter Seven

"Dung weevils!" Jane kicked the stall door in frustration. She had gone to the stables to practice one of Jester's silly walks. But it wasn't working. She felt stiff and wooden instead of loose and floppy.

"Practice makes perfect," she told herself. And she tried again.

She was midway through trying to walk like a goose when she heard Gunther and Dragon laughing out in the driveway. She felt a sudden thrill of delight. Had they spotted her? Was she really funny after all?

She looked up, and her spirits sagged.

They hadn't even seen her — they were too busy telling each other more of their silly jokes.

"Wait for me," she yelled, hurrying to catch them. "I want to hear your jokes."

Gunther dismissed her with a snort. "I doubt it, Jane. That would take a sense of humor. The last time I looked, yours had been stolen by villains."

Dragon stared at Jane. "Is this true?"

Jane started to protest, then realized she was being serious again. She forced herself to laugh.

"Very funny, Gunther. Maybe we should all go on patrol and rescue my poor sense of humor." She laughed again and thumped Gunther on the back. "Saddle up, Squire. We shall hunt down those thieves together."

Gunther sighed and shook his head. "Overdoing it, Jane."

"Better still," said Jane with a laugh, "we can take a spade and dig a pit. We can trap them and rescue my poor sense of humor. Yes. Good plan." Finally, Jane stopped babbling and looked up. But no one was laughing. She felt a wave of panic. Why was it so hard to be funny? And why was everyone good at it except her? Even Pepper had a better sense of humor.

"Oh, Pepper told me a joke," she tried again. "Want to hear it?"

"A joke?" said Dragon, swinging around to face her like an eager puppy. "Oh, yes. I always knew this day would come. Come on, then. Tell it! Tell it!" He wagged his long green tail with excitement.

Jane cleared her throat and tried to remember how the joke had started.

"This is going to be good," Dragon said, already chuckling. "Oh, yes. Watch out, ribs, you are going to HURT!"

"I know," said Jane, suddenly

remembering. "What sits on a toilet seat in Gaul?"

Dragon kept smiling as he waited for the punch line.

"A royal turd!" said Jane.

"Is that it?" asked Dragon.

Gunther grinned and shook his head sadly.

"I think it was," Jane said. She wanted the cobblestones to give way beneath her. She wanted to tumble through into the dungeons and never be seen again.

"Right. So anyway, I should go," she said. "I have a busy day. Busy, busy." She turned and hurried away as quickly as she could, relieved that her flame-red hair would be hiding the bright red of her neck.

Chapter Eight

Jane strode into the yard. It was time for sword practice, and she was in the mood for a good workout.

"Jane, are you cross with me?" came a voice from above her. She looked up. Dragon sat lazing on his wall above the yard.

"What would I be cross about?" Jane asked.

"Exactly what I was thinking," said Dragon. "What has my little short-life friend got to be so huffy about?"

Jane laughed. How did he do that? How did he always know how she felt? He was right, of course; she was cross.

Cross because Dragon seemed to be enjoying Gunther's company more than hers today. Cross because only Gunther could make him laugh. But most of all she was cross for feeling so jealous. Jealousy was a weakness. And there was no place for weakness in a knight.

Gunther strolled into the yard. "Hey, Dragon. What's brown and floppy and barks like a dog?"

Dragon smiled. He knew this one. "A poodle. A poo-doll."

Gunther laughed and took his stance in front of Jane. He planted his feet at right angles and held his blade up straight before his face. He was a master of the correct stance, especially when Sir Theodore was watching from the balcony above.

"A poo-doll. Get it, Jane?" Gunther whispered so Sir Theodore wouldn't hear. "Oh, wait. I forgot. You have no funny bone, do you?"

"I have plenty of bones, Gunther," she whispered back at him. "And right now all of them are waiting to dance rings around you. Are you ready for a whipping?"

"Now, that really is a joke," hissed Gunther.

Sir Theodore stepped forward to the balcony rail. "Are you ready, squires?"

They nodded, their eyes locking on each other.

"Then listen carefully," said the

elderly knight. "Today you will focus your blows on the opponent's arms. In true combat, a knight's leathers will stop a blade from cutting through, but the blow will tire the arm beneath. And a knight who cannot lift a sword is a beaten knight. Are we clear on this?"

"Very clear, Sir Theodore," yelled Gunther.

"Clear," said Jane.

"Then await my command. Turn your blades as you strike, and keep the blows soft and flat."

And so it began. They used light wooden swords with no points. Yet a well-placed stroke with the flat of the blade could sting.

Gunther made the first strike. But Jane was ready for him, sweeping her blade down to block his attack. Gunther was surprised. He was even more surprised when Jane swung around on the spot, bringing her sword to his unprotected side. She stopped it an inch before contact, then tapped Gunther softly above the elbow.

"Woohoo! Go, Coppertop!" yelled Dragon.

Gunther managed to keep the grin on his face.

"Is that the best you can do, Jane?"

"No, Gunther. I would never waste

my best moves on you. But then I never have to."

And with that she advanced, delivering a flurry of steady blows. Gunther was forced backward. He managed a countermove, lunging at Jane.

But he overreached. Jane saw her chance. She sidestepped. Gunther lost his balance as Jane stuck out a foot to trip him headfirst into the dirt.

"Gunther. How can I keep scoring points if you lie around down there?" She leaned forward, offering him a hand. Gunther reached up to take it, then fell back when Jane withdrew it.

Gunther glared at her. "What was that about?"

"That was a joke, Gunther. I know how much you like a good joke."

"Thank you, squires," called Sir Theodore. "That will be enough for today. Jane, could I have a word, please?"

Jane ran through the stables, through the workshop, and up the wooden steps that led to the knight's quarters.

Sir Theodore was standing near the window. He seemed distracted, almost stern.

"Jane, you were aggressive in your practice today."

"Thank you, Sir Theodore."

"That was not a compliment. I am disappointed."

Jane was confused. She had beaten her opponent. She had followed the rules and made light touches to his arms. She doubted Gunther had a single bruise, except to his ego.

"Where did I go wrong, Sir Theodore?"

"Jane, I must teach you skills that will make you a warrior. Not just in the arena, but also in life. You took a grudge into practice today, did you not?"

"I think I did, Sir Theodore."

"I know you did. What was on your mind?"

Jane hung her head. "I was angry with Gunther. He has been trying to make friends with Dragon."

"Jealousy, Jane?" The old knight looked surprised. "I expect better from you. Having a fellow squire on good terms with your dragon would be in the King's interests, would it not?"

"I suppose so. But how can I trust Gunther to be careful of Dragon's feelings? How can I trust him to—?"

"Enough, Jane! You are both knights in training. It is not for you to judge him."

Jane had seldom been spoken to this harshly by Sir Theodore. She hurried from the room, her face burning with shame. But as she stomped down the stairs, her shame soon turned to anger—anger at herself.

How could she let jealousy get in the way of her training? She was better than that, or she wanted to be. It was time to swallow her pride and apologize to Gunther.

Chapter Nine

*J*ane found Jester in the garden, juggling onions. "Jester, would you be my audience? I need you to hear something and tell me if it works. It has to be sincere."

"Of course." Jester caught the onions and bowed to his friend. "One genius tutor at your service."

Jane took a deep breath and began. "Gunther, I have behaved badly. And not in the best tradition of the Knights' Code." She paused to check on Jester's reaction. Her friend raised an eyebrow and said nothing. Jane carried on.

"So it is with my most sincere apology that I ask for your forgiveness. And for the opportunity to regain your trust and your friendship."

She stopped and smiled. "Well? What do you think?"

Jester bent over, laughing. "Yes, oh, yes, Jane. Hilarious! True comedy, well done. Very funny!"

Jane stared at him. "I was being serious," she said, and stormed off to find Gunther. If she couldn't get the apology exactly right, at least she could get it over with.

As Jane headed for the main gate, she spotted her father in a heated discussion with the Merchant. Jane stepped into the shadows and waited.

If her father saw her, he might load her up with boring jobs.

From her hiding place, Jane could hear bits of their discussion. It was about the price of stone. And there was only one place to buy good stone. From the Merchant's quarry.

"The royal family is your most regular customer," Jane's father was saying. "We need the stone for our renovations, but these prices are an outrage."

"Indeed, indeed." The Merchant nodded. "But my own costs keep rising. The labor for cutting the stone, the horse and wagon for transport."

Watching this horrible man cheat her father made Jane's blood boil. Sometimes she wished she could break

the law rather than uphold it. Just for once she would like to use her big green friend to teach this greedy bog weevil a lesson.

"Very well," said her father, "we shall pay your new price. But it will tax the King's pleasure and his purse."

The two men nodded and parted company. The Merchant strode off, his face smug. Jane turned to go but stopped when she saw Gunther striding in through the main gate. She drew in a deep breath—it was apology time.

But the Merchant saw Gunther too, and called out, "Ah, Gunther. Come here, boy!"

Jane slipped into the stables and crouched down behind the open door.

"What is it, Father?" sighed Gunther. "More chores?"

"Perhaps," replied the Merchant in a hushed voice, "though not for you. How close a leash do you have on that wretched lizard?"

"You mean Dragon?" asked Gunther.

"Of course I mean Dragon. Would the disgusting creature run an errand for you?"

Jane felt the blood pulse in her sword arm. Training to be a knight was a wonderful challenge, but it had sharpened her body's reaction to danger. She forced herself to stay calm and keep out of sight.

"I suppose he might," said Gunther. "We have become good friends of late."

The Merchant grinned and draped an arm over his son's shoulder. "Then you must ask him, Gunther. I have another load of barrels that need delivery to the wharf."

Gunther nodded. "No harm in asking," he said. "It would save time, and it would save my poor back."

"And my pocket," the Merchant said with a laugh. "So keep making friends with him, boy. He could prove very helpful with our debt collecting as well. Nothing like the threat of burning crops to make our farmers pay up on time. And let's not forget that boulder I showed you at the quarry."

"The boulder, Father?"

"I need it delivered to the castle. Once your friend has done the barrels, have him drop it outside the back wall. The fall will shatter the boulder and save the cost of splitting it. That lizard will make us a fortune."

"But Father, that boulder is huge! Should we push our luck with Dragon?"

"Luck!" scoffed the Merchant. "Luck has nothing to do with it! Brains will beat dragon muscle every time!"

Watching from her hiding place, Jane bubbled with anger. She could hardly believe it. No, that wasn't true. It was very easy to believe. She had never trusted Gunther.

Jane hurried off to warn Dragon. She would have to be careful how she did it. If the big newt lost his temper, things could turn ugly. Jane was cross with Gunther, but not cross enough to see him turned into a stick of charcoal.

Chapter Ten

Dragon broke into a silly grin when he saw Jane. "Where have you been?" he asked. "Not still huffy with me, are you?"

"No, Dragon. Not with you. Now, sit down, I have something difficult to tell you."

Dragon groaned. "Go on, then," he said, sighing. "It must be serious."

Jane glared at him. "It is. How did you know?"

"Because your hands are on your hips. And you always put your hands on your hips when you are going to be boring and serious. You get it from your mother."

"I do not!"

But he was right. Her hands were crunched into fists and planted on her hips. Exactly like her mother.

"Yes, well, it is serious, Dragon. And you are not to go blowing off steam, or flame. Is that clear?"

"Yes, Miss Huffy Cross Person."

"Good. Well, I heard Gunther talking to his father. They want to use you to do all their dirty work for them."

Dragon frowned at her. "Perhaps you misheard them?"

"No." Jane shook her head firmly. "The Merchant was very pleased with himself!"

Dragon pushed himself up and stood over her. His silly puppy-dog

look had vanished. Instead, he looked disappointed. "Jane, enough!"

"What? Do you think I would make this up?"

"No. I think your judgment is clouded. Even Sir Theodore said so!"

"How do you know that? Were you eavesdropping?"

"Yes. I was worried about you! I

thought my *friend* was in trouble!"

"I *am* your friend."

"Yes. A huffy, jealous friend who thinks I could be fooled by a couple of short-lives!"

"Dragon!"

"Well, I have better things to do than be lectured to by a huffy, puffy friend. Call me when you have something friendly to talk about." And away Dragon flew, up over the wall and out of the castle.

Jane scolded herself. She had handled that badly. Worse than badly! Dragon could be a complete beef-head sometimes. And now when Gunther asked for help, Dragon would give it to him rather than admit he was wrong.

Chapter Eleven

"Dragon! Over here!" Gunther had spotted Dragon leaving the castle and waved him over. The young squire was standing beside another pile of barrels that needed carting to the wharf.

Dragon circled for a moment, then landed beside him. "What is it? Want a game of bandyball, do you?"

Gunther made a show of straightening his back as if it were sore from overwork. "Sorry, Dragon. I wish I could. But I have to get this salted herring down to the wharf."

"Wait—I know!" said Dragon. "We could go and listen to the cows."

He closed his eyes, pushed out his lips, and mooed. "*Moo.* Sheer genius. Starts with *mmm* and ends in *ooo*. Completely brilliant. How do they do it?"

"No idea," said Gunther, laughing. "I wish I could come and listen to them with you, Dragon. But alas, this is going to keep me busy for a while."

Gunther bent to lift a barrel and threw Dragon a sideways glance. "Of course, I would finish the work a lot sooner if someone were to lend me a hand. . . ."

Dragon hesitated, a flicker of doubt crossing his face. Then he grinned and bowled Gunther out of the way. "Move over, short-life. I shall be back in two shakes of a magnificent tail!" He picked

up an entire chain of barrels and took off toward the wharf.

Gunther quietly congratulated himself. "Father was right! That *was* easy."

Chapter Twelve

"*I* am a complete maggot-brain, Jester. I really messed it up."

Jester sat at the picnic table, strumming his lute. Jane paced up and down in front of him.

"Even Dragon thinks I acted out of jealousy!"

"And did you?"

"Yes. Just a little. But I heard what I heard."

"Maybe you should leave them to sort it out. Dragon is nobody's fool. Except yours. For you, he can be a clown."

Jester was right. Dragon was smart enough to see through any scheme of

Gunther's. Jane stopped pacing. She looked out beyond the castle walls and let out a sigh.

Then she spotted something. Something that made her mad. It was Dragon! And he was hauling a chain of barrels into the air. "That does it!" she said. "The silly newt has fallen for it!

Gunther is using him like a pack mule!"

Jane turned and raced off. Nobody was going to treat her friend like that. Nobody!

Jane fumed as she strode down the cobbled street to the village square. She could see Gunther and his father laughing together, and it made her boil. How could Gunther do this?

She doubled her pace just as the Merchant turned and spotted her. The man whispered something in his son's ear and walked off into his house.

"Where is he, Gunther?" snapped Jane, barely able to contain her anger.

"Who? My father? You just missed him."

"Dragon, you beef-wit! I saw him doing your donkey work just now. How much are you paying him?"

Gunther put a finger to his chin and stared at the sky as if doing the sums. "Oh, let me see. What would be a fair wage? You tell me, Jane. What do you pay to be flown out on patrol every day?"

"What? That is completely different!"

"Oh, really. How? How is it different? Dragon does your bidding no matter what you ask of him. And you pay him nothing, not a single coin."

Jane was completely at a loss. "Because Dragon wants to help me. As a friend!"

"Exactly!" exclaimed Gunther. "Just as Dragon is helping me now. As a friend." He folded his arms and grinned at Jane. He had won the argument, and he knew it.

A shadow spread across the ground as Dragon flew down to join them. "Hello, Jane. Come to help, have you?"

"To help? Yes, if you need it. Do you need help?"

"No, my little short-life. The work is done. We can all go and watch the cows."

"Not right now, thank you, Dragon. I came by to tell you something."

"Oh. What would that be? Nothing too huffy, I hope." Dragon narrowed his eyes. Gunther folded his arms and waited, a thin smile on his face.

"Yes, Jane. What have you come to

tell him? Another joke perhaps? A funny one this time? Oh, wait; I know. Tell Dragon the joke about the girl with egg on her face."

Jane ignored him. "I just came here to . . . er . . . to apologize. I have been very boring lately."

Dragon shook his head. "No, Jane, you have been completely boring. Trust me. When you have lived for three hundred years, you get to be an expert on boring. And you, Miss Hands-on-Hips, have almost broken the record!"

"All right, you big frog," said Jane, bursting into laughter. "Look, I came to apologize. And to tell you how much I've missed spending time with you."

"Completely understandable." Dragon buffed his claws on his chest. "I am the very best company anyone could wish for. Except for cows; they are strangely shy with me. But we should go and see them, anyway."

"Count me in," said Gunther. Then he paused and tried to appear casual. "But before we go, could you do one small favor for me? Very small."

Dragon leaned in toward Gunther. The puppy-dog smile was still on his face, but Jane could see a spark in his eyes. A dangerous spark.

"A little favor?" asked Dragon, stepping forward and pressing his face close to Gunther's. "Just what kind of teeny-weeny favor might this be?"

"Erm, well. There is a small boulder that needs to be moved to the castle." Gunther tried to step away from the hot, smoky breath. But his way was

blocked by the empty wagon parked behind him. "Only if you want to, Dragon. It is in Father's quarry, just north of here, and . . ."

"I know where it is," said Dragon softly. "I know every rock and boulder around the castle. Do you want to know how?"

Gunther nodded.

"I know because I fly over them every day with my friend, Jane. When we are on patrol protecting the kingdom from thieves and villains!" He hissed the last word very quietly, right in Gunther's face. A thread of smoke drifted into Gunther's eyes, and they began to water.

Jane stepped forward. This was

exactly what she'd been afraid of. It took a lot to make Dragon angry, but if someone pushed him too far, then no one, not even Jane, could stop him from doing something foolish.

"Dragon, you should rest before you do anything else. Anything you might regret."

"Rest?" whispered Dragon. "No, I am never too tired to do a small favor for a friend. A boulder, you say? No problem." And, with a soft growl, he turned away.

"Wait," said Jane.

"No. I have to fetch a teeny-weeny boulder for my teeny-weeny short-life friend here."

"I understand," said Jane, and she

planted herself in his way. "But I want to stop my very large friend from making a teeny-weeny mistake he will regret."

Dragon said nothing. He sighed and stooped down so Jane could scramble onto his neck. And with a great flapping of wings, they flew off into the late-afternoon sky.

Chapter Thirteen

The air whipped Jane's hair from her face as they climbed steeply.

"Are you still angry with me?" she asked.

"No, just disappointed. You thought Gunther had me fooled, but I was onto him all the time."

"Of course you were."

"I was! And now he will pay the price."

"What price? Gunther behaved badly. But that is no excuse to take matters into your own hands."

"Claws, Jane. Into my own claws."

"Even worse. Promise you will

do nothing painful to Gunther."

"Painful? No. I shall hardly feel a thing." Dragon dropped into a steep dive. He had spotted the large boulder.

The boulder was heavy. Very heavy—even for a creature as strong as Dragon. But by doubling his wing beats, he managed to take off with it.

"Now what?" asked Jane as Dragon struggled to gain more height. "Are you planning to drop it on their house?"

"Drop it? No. But it might accidentally slip from my clumsy claws."

"And it might accidentally kill someone!"

"Life can be so cruel! Never mind— places to go, boulders to drop."

"Dragon! I know how you feel. You thought he was a friend, and it hurts when a friend lets you down. But squashing Gunther with a boulder will not make you feel better."

"It might."

Jane leaned forward and tried to catch his eye. "Listen, you big frog! When we get upset, we make bad decisions. And this is a very bad decision!"

"No, Jane. This is a brilliant decision. Where is the harm in squashing Gunther like a ripe tomato? Splat!"

"The harm? Quite a bit to Gunther, I should think. And to me. I thought I was losing my best friend when you two were off laughing at your silly jokes. But I really will lose you if you do this. Squashing one of the King's subjects is an act of war. You will be banished from the kingdom forever."

Dragon was silent for a moment. He glanced back at her, dipped his head, and dropped into a steep dive.

"Sorry," he roared as the wind rushed past. "But those two need a lesson."

Chapter Fourteen

"*E*xcellent work, boy." The Merchant stood at the wharf beside a tall stack of barrels. He turned to his son and gave him a pat on the head. "Your lizard made a quick job of this. That stupid beast is going to save us a lot of money."

But Gunther wasn't listening. He was watching a big streak of green lizard swooping down toward them.

"Hey, Gunther!" yelled Dragon. "Fancy a game of Catch-a-Very-Big-Rock?"

As Dragon swept low over the wharf, he released the boulder just inches from the ground. It tumbled,

end over end, like a giant bowling ball—straight at Gunther and the Merchant.

"Jump!" screamed Gunther, pushing his father and diving out of the way. The boulder crashed into the stack of barrels, scattering them like ninepins. The force of the blow smashed four of them to pieces. They splintered like matchwood, and the salted herring inside them scattered all over the wharf. The other barrels went tumbling off the wharf and into the water.

Gunther stood up and grinned at the mess. "Well, Father. That was a very good shot for such a stupid beast."

Still sprawled on his stomach, the Merchant glared up at his son. "What is so funny, boy? This has cost us a month's profit."

But Gunther couldn't help himself. The sight of his father on his knees, turning purple with rage, was too much for him. He burst into a fit of the giggles and had to clamp a hand over his mouth.

Jane and Dragon circled back overhead, and Gunther gave them a small wave. Then he ran off along the wharf before his giggles turned into a hopeless laughing fit.

"Poor Gunther," said Jane. "He is going to have a list of jobs as long as his father's face when this is over."

"Good," said Dragon. "He deserves it."

"Maybe. I just hope you were trying to miss them with that boulder."

Dragon shook his head and looked hurt. "If I had been trying to hit them, they would be lying in the water right now."

"And it *was* fun," Jane said, laughing.

"As funny as dung?"

"Oh, yes. Just as funny as dung.

Come on, you big newt. We have an evening patrol to do."

And away they soared, climbing into the warm red sky.

"What do you call a cow with no legs?" asked Dragon.

"Is this another of your bad jokes?"

"Yes. Ground beef." Dragon laughed so hard, he could barely keep in the air.

"I know one," said Jane.

"Oh, dear, is it as good as all your other jokes? That is to say, is it horribly bad?"

"Thank you for the encouragement."

"As tragically bad and unfunny as every other joke you have ruined since the day you started telling bad jokes?"

"I expect so. Do you want to hear it?"

"Call me stupid, but yes, please."

"OK, why did the cow jump over the moon?"

Dragon raised an eyebrow and waited for the punch line.

"Because the farmer had cold hands," said Jane, smiling, pleased to have remembered a whole joke.

"Not bad," said Dragon. "Not funny. But not completely awful."

"Thank you."

"So. How do you make milk shake?"

Jane shrugged and then held on for dear life as Dragon plunged toward a herd of cows. The animals broke into a mad, racing panic and charged all over their field.

"Like that!" yelled Dragon.

And away they flew, spinning and rolling above the cows, with Jane clinging tight to the neck of her very best friend.

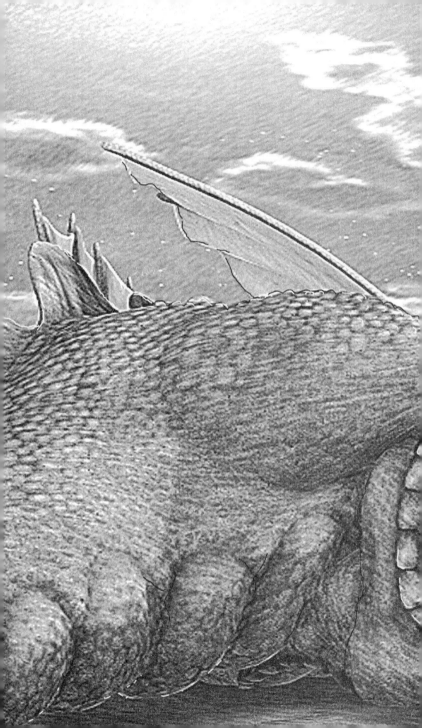

About the Author

MARTIN BAYNTON always wanted to be a writer and illustrator. At school, he used to get into trouble for drawing cartoons of his teachers, and his best grades were always for his story writing. Yet his first books weren't published until he was thirty. Up until then, he was too busy traveling the world and having adventures of his own. Martin lives with his wife on a small farm in Australia. They have two grown-up children, two dogs, and three horses. For the last four years, Martin has been working with Weta Productions in New Zealand, turning his *Jane and the Dragon* books into an award-winning television series.